I0784059

The Village Has Changed

Written by Sun Yu
Illustrated by Yang Bo
Translated from the Chinese by Helen Wang

New Classic Press

2024

Yucun is a small village surrounded on three sides by mountains covered with bamboo. When Xiaolin was born here, there was a small bamboo forest at the back of his house.

3

Every morning, Xiaolin and his mother would go into the bamboo forest to collect eggs.

The BOOM at the end of the village sent the hens into a panic. But Xiaolin knew it meant that work had started at the mine.

When the mine and cement factory opened in Yucun, many villagers stopped doing what they used to do, and became workers.

Xiaolin's father worked in the cement factory at the end of the village.

He used to come home from work covered in dust.

It wasn't just the grown-ups that changed, the whole village seemed to change.

As soon as Xiaolin could walk, he used to play with his friends in the bamboo forest. He loved swinging on the bamboo, until it got covered in dust and made him choke and sneeze.

Big trucks filled with rocks clattered about all day long.

They made pits and potholes in the village roads, and tossed out stones and earth so randomly that Xiaolin and his friends couldn't dodge them all.

The number of factories in the village grew.
Filthy dust filled the air, and got everywhere.
Xiaolin's mother was constantly having to fetch a
cloth and wipe it away.

When Xiaolin went to secondary school, he still went to the bambo
forest, but it was not a place to play games, as the bamboo was rottin.

Polluted water from the factories poured into the little strean
which turned yellow and stank. Crops and vegetables didn't gro
properly, and sold for next to nothing. Xiaolin's mother made bambo
baskets and dustpans to help make ends meet. Xiaolin learned how t
make them too.

"You're good with your hands, better than me," his mother praise
him.

Sometimes Xiaolin would make a bamboo toy, perhaps a pretty bird or a dragonfly, and give it to a friend. He was delighted when people called him a bamboo master craftsman. "I'd like to open a shop one day, and sell the pieces I've made," he said.

When his mother said he would never earn a living that way, he kept quiet, but held the dream deep in his heart.

When Xiaolin finished middle school, Yucun was even dirtier and more chaotic than before.

The factories were closing, and many people now chose to leave the village. Like them, Xiaolin took the bus to the city and became a migrant worker.

Xiaolin worked in the city for a few years. Life was hard. When he wasn't working in a noisy factory, he was weaving through traffic jams on crowded streets. He missed the village, and he missed the old bamboo forest.

While he was away, the village began to change. And every time he went home, he discovered it was changing in wonderful ways.

As the cloud of grey dust started to lift, the sky gradually turned blue.

Little by little, the roads became flatter and cleaner.

Now when it rained, people could hear their shoes slapping on the firm, new road.

They didn't get muddy, as they used to before.

Silt and rubbish were gradually
cleared from the stream.

20

Year by year, the water grew clearer. Slowly, the fish returned.

The land was able to support crops and vegetables again. The villagers made little gardens beside their houses.

22

They planted different kinds of flowers that
bloomed at different times of the year.

The migrant workers came back from the city.
They renovated their old houses and turned them
into homestays.

Birds came back too, and
started building nests.

By this time, the mine and factories had been closed for a long time.

The village was getting greener and greener, and the air smelled clean and fresh, of earth and grass. Xiaolin felt his village had improved so much!

Tourists started coming to Yucun. They took photos of the village, enjoyed the village food, and had a lovely time. This motivated the villagers to do more.

When Xiaolin brought his son Qiqi back to the village he saw Uncle Yang, a village official, tending the old apricot tree in front of his house.

"Xiaolin, look around you! A lot of young people have come back, some are opening homestays, some are planting vegetables."

He smiled at Xiaolin, "Business is good! Why don't you come back? You could do whatever you like. The village will support you and help you."

Xiaolin started to think about it.

Xiaolin could see how much Qiqi loved playing with bamboo toys, and remembered his childhood dream.

He discussed the idea of returning to the village with his wife. She agreed, and they were both filled with hope for the future.

By the time the yellow rapesee
flowers opened the following sprin
Xiaolin's old house had been renovate

Xiaolin opened his shop, and filled every space with bamboo goods that he had made himself.

When Qiqi's friends from the city came to visit, he took them by the hand and showed them round. "My dad made this!" "And he made that too!" he said proudly. "Our village is a Tourism Village. It's even been on TV!"

Xiaolin was also very proud. He had never imagined that the village could be so beautiful, or that his childhood dream could come true.

When Xiaolin had time, he liked to go into the bamboo forest.

Qiqi liked to go too.

"Dad, I want to swing on the bamboo, just like you when you were little!"

The sound of Qiqi's laughter and the rustling of the bamboo rose up, then settled quietly in Xiaolin's heart.

Xiaolin knew that he would never leave Yucun again.
This little village surrounded by bamboo was his home.

"Nature & Me" Series

The Village Has Changed

Written by Sun Yu
Illustrated by Yang Bo
Translated from the Chinese by Helen Wang

First Published in Chinese by Phoenix Juvenile and Children's Publishing Ltd., 2023
English Copyright ©2024 New Classic Press
Through arrangement with Phoenix Juvenile and Children's Publishing Ltd.

ISBN 978-1-915865-73-1
Printed in the United Kingdom of Great Britain and Northern Ireland

10 9 8 7 6 5 4 3 2 1

The publisher's policy is to use paper manufactured from sustainable forests.

This book is about a rea[l] village in China, and the mai[n] character is modelled on a rea[l] person. Thank you to Mr H[u] Qingfa of Yucun village, Anj[i] county, Zhejiang province, fo[r] sharing his family's experience[s] and feelings.

In 2021 the United Nation[s] World Tourism Organizatio[n] (UNWTO) named Yucun as [a] Best Tourism Village, calling i[t] an example for environmenta[l] recovery.

www.ingramcontent.com/pod-product-compliance
Lightning Source LLC
Chambersburg PA
CBHW041156300726
48981CB00004B/272